THIS BOOK =
5 MEALS FOR
A CHILD IN NEED

2015

To Leighton, Brooks, and Crosbie

Special Thanks to Molly Watts

Merry Christmas Addison!
We love you so much!
Papa and Ge

LIGHT UP THE DARKNESS

WRITTEN BY DREW BREAUX

ILLUSTRATED BY CHELSEA KENNA

I was just a boy one winter's night

Beneath my favorite tree...

It was the night of my 12th birthday

All alone as I could be

No cards, no cake, no candles

No presents wrapped for me...

Because no one threw a party

For a little boy who couldn't see

I sat there like most nights before,

Wishing the darkness would light up for me

When in my ear a voice came near,

And I wondered, "who could it be?"

I heard the stress in his voice

As he pleaded for a room...

A place to stay for he, his wife,

And the baby in her womb

"There's no place for you here!"

He was told again and once more...

Those words I'd heard enough myself

To not knock on anyone's door

With no place left to go

They shuffled closer to my tree...

A family of only two who were

Soon to become three

His very first cry was sharp and shrill...
I could feel the animals scurry

His parents laughed...and then they cried
And softly whispered, *"don't you worry"*

And suddenly the night was gleaming

Beneath my sightless eyes...

As if someone chose the brightest star

And plucked it right down from the skies

One by one they came to see Him,

Their songs made their way to my tree...

They called him names like "Lord" and "Savior",

Said He'd light up the dark for all to see...

I could smell that some were shepherds,

I heard voices in the sky

Singing, "peace on earth, goodwill to men,

Glory to God on high!"

But soon the singing turned to silence,

I was sure that they'd moved on...

I hoped He *was* the Prince of Peace...

The Messiah God's own son

Then the wind blew for a while...

And the nights felt dark again...

Thirty years had come and gone

Since that night beneath my tree...

I'd traded in my shaded spot,

For a place by the road to plea

Day after day I sat and hoped

The darkness would light up for me...

When in my ear a crowd came near

And I wondered, "who could it be?"

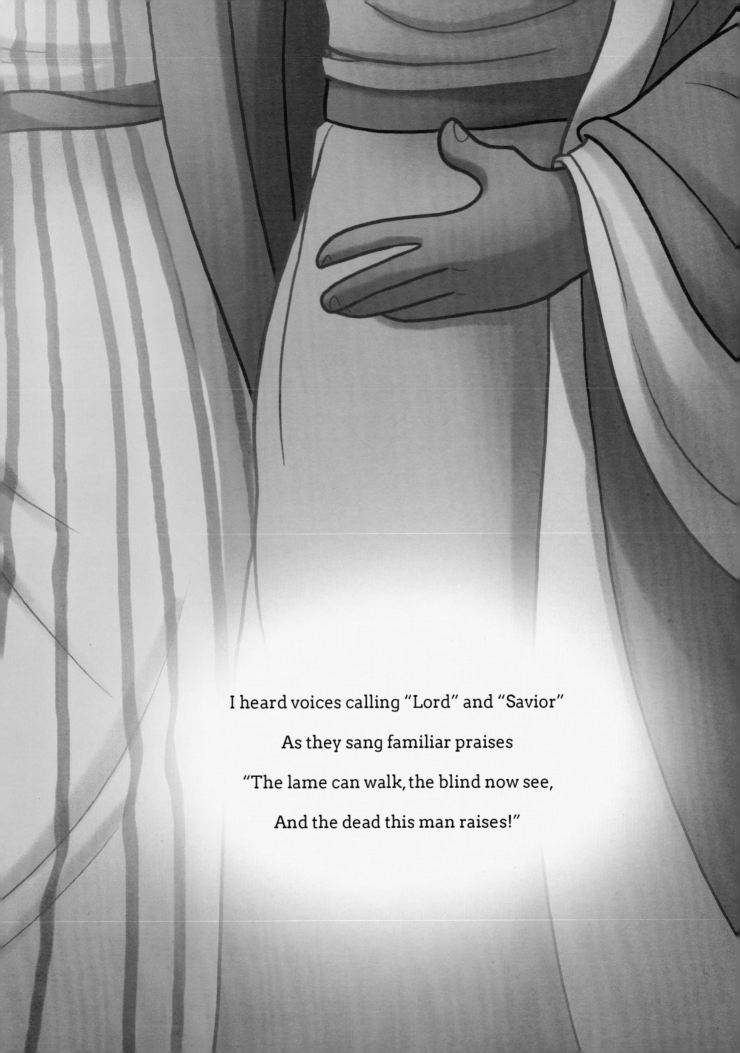

I heard voices calling "Lord" and "Savior"

As they sang familiar praises

"The lame can walk, the blind now see,

And the dead this man raises!"

So with all of my might I called His name,

And He took my hand, He noticed me...

With just a touch He lit up the darkness,

He opened my eyes so I could see!

The little baby born that night
As I listened to his cries...
Now listened to my humble cry
And gave sight to sightless eyes

That's why they called Him "Light of the world"

That night beneath my tree...

'Cause He was born to light up the darkness

For ones like you and me

NOT
THE END...

ONLY THE BEGINNING!